A FOOL'S LIFE

芥川龍之介

AKUTAGAWA RYŪNOSUKE

A FOOL'S LIFE

ARU AHŌ NO ISSHŌ

Translated from the Japanese by

ANTHONY BARNETT

& TORAIWA NAOKO

A·B

Translated from the Japanese
ARU AHŌ NO ISSHŌ
first published in the October 1927 issue of *Kaizō*

This English translation
A FOOL'S LIFE
Copyright © Allardyce, Barnett, Publishers 2007

Published 2007 by Allardyce Book
imprint of
Allardyce, Barnett, Publishers
14 Mount Street, Lewes, East Sussex BN7 1HL England
www.abar.net

Distributed in the USA by SPD Inc
1341 Seventh Street, Berkeley CA 94710-1403
www.spdbooks.org

Typeset by AB ©omposer
in Centaur MT
under the guidance of the
Half-Human Half-Horse Gods of 16. Pillow
Japanese cover titling in Kozuka Minchō
Printed by ARowe in EUK

*Page 8 shows the page of Akutagawa's manuscript with title and
discarded titles in The Literary Museum of Yamanashi Prefecture
Manuscript pages for sections 37, 41, 45 are shown on pages 45, 49, 53
Frontispiece photo of Akutagawa at his writing desk July 1924 in
Akutagawa Ryūnosoke: Shinchō Japanese Literature Album
Sekiguchi Yasuyoshi, ed., Tokyo, Shinchōsha, 1983
Cover emblem by Anthony Barnett*

CIP records for this book are available from
The British Library and The Library of Congress

ISBN 978 0 907954 35 4

IT IS tempting to think of translating the title of this posthumously published work by Akutagawa along the lines *Episodes in a Fool's Life* or *Scenes from a Fool's Life*, for both are something of what they are, in order to come close to the syllable count of the original *Aru ahō no isshō*—in fact, Akutagawa tried out three other titles, which he discarded: "His Dream", "Biographical Esquisse", "The Myth"—but it would be a mistake. For Akutagawa approaching his death this is his life, not merely selected episodes or created scenes in it. His life passing in front of his eyes.

One might assume that syllable count is what the translator of the 2006 Penguin Akutagawa selection *Rashōmon and Seventeen Other Stories* had in mind when he titled his version *The Life of a Stupid Man*. But there is more to that wrong tone. There the close of Akutagawa's accompanying letter is given "laugh at my stupidity." Here I give "laugh at how foolish I am." A moot point? I don't think so. Akutagawa may have thought he was a fool—among other characterizations such as the motley puppet with which he compares himself in 35—and a man afraid of going mad or that he had already done so but he was not stupid. He did not say he was stupid. It is equally possible to differentiate in English and Japanese uses of such words. Stupidity more than foolishness is an antithesis of intelligence and Akutagawa was vastly intelligent. One can joke about being intelligent but stupid or coarsely command an intelligence not to be stupid—let us not complicate matters with idiotic or silly—but that is not what Akutagawa does. *A Fool's Life* is neither joke—do not be misled by "laugh" in the letter—nor coarse. It is as serious as Akutagawa's life and death. Should further evidence be needed for sensible "fool" not insensitive "stupid" turn to the note to 25. "Strindberg".

Three English versions and a French version have come my way: *A Fool's Life* translated by Will Petersen first appeared in *Caterpillar* magazine (New York, April–July 1968), widely disseminated since, apparently without revision. It was reprinted in de luxe book form with etchings as *A Fool's Life* (Tokyo, Mushinsha / New York, Grossman, 1970). It was further reprinted in *Hell Screen, Cogwheels, A Fool's Life* (various translators, Hygiene, Colorado, Eridanos, 1987), which is the edition known to me. Among later reprints it is included in *The Essential Akutagawa* (New York, Marsilio, 1999).

The second English version appeared at a late stage in the progress of my own. It is the aforementioned *The Life of a Stupid Man* in *Rashōmon and Seventeen Other Stories* translated by Jay Rubin (London, Penguin, 2006).

The French version is included in *La vie d'un idiot et autres nouvelles* translated by Edwige de Chavanes (Paris, Gallimard, 1987). "Idiot", with "rire de mon idiotie", will do in French in a way that it will not in English, though the immediate reference to Strindberg's "fou" is lost, notwithstanding that it came to Akutagawa as "fool" not "madman"—see again note to 25.

The third English version, announced as *The Life of an Idiot* included in the Akutagawa selection *Mandarins* translated by Charles de Wolf (New York, Archipelago, 2007), was set to appear as the present volume went to press.

A number of other autobiographical pieces complement *A Fool's Life*, notably *Haguruma* also written shortly before Akutagawa's death. It treats much the same material but very differently in a troubled complex six-part narrative. There are at least five English translations of which it is a good idea to read more than one: by Beongcheon Yu as "The Cogwheel" in *Chicago Review*, xviii/2 (1965); by Cid Corman and Kamaike Susumu as "Cogwheels" (New York, New Directions, 1974), reprinted in the aforementioned Eridanos and Marsilio editions; by Howard Norman in *Cogwheels and Other Stories* (Oakville, Ontario, Mosaic/Valley, 1982); by Jay Rubin as *Spinning Gears*, in the aforementioned 2006 Penguin selection; by Charles de Wolf announced as "Cogwheels" in the 2007 Archipelago selection; and a French version by Edwige de Chavanes as *Engrenage* in the 1987 Gallimard selection.

Hell Screen also reprints Yu's translation of Akutagawa's last testament "A Note to a Certain Old Friend", first printed in Beongcheon Yu, *Akutagawa: An Introduction* (Detroit, Wayne State University Press, 1972). Its addressee, Kume Masao, released it to the press immediately after Akutagawa's death. It talks about *A Fool's Life* but it is not the letter to Kume printed here. Yu's volume also includes a few translated extracts from *The Life of a Fool*—Yu's title. Some other related pieces, translated for the first time in the 2006 Penguin selection, are mentioned in the notes to the present volume.

I printed an earlier version of 37, here titled, not without reservations, "One from Yonder", as "The Northlander" as an epigraph to the "New Poems" section of *Miscanthus: Selected and New Poems* (Exeter, Shearsman, 2005) but my translation there was wrong on several counts. Doubtless there are greater or lesser improvements still to be made elsewhere.

I must let others judge the merits or otherwise of my translation but if I am to cite feet-on-the-ground models of theory and practice—quite at odds with other English versions, one of which is mischievous—I would draw the interested reader's attention to Umberto Eco's *Experiences in Translation* (Toronto, Toronto University Press, 2001) and *Mouse or Rat? Translation as Negotiation* (London, Weidenfeld & Nicholson, 2003). The latter happens to be remarkably appropriate given a particular word in 24. "Childbirth" commented on in the notes.

I owe whatever good approach I may have found for *A Fool's Life* to Dr TORAIWA NAOKO, Professor of English at Meiji University, Tokyo. Dr Toraiwa has worked tirelessly through many drafts, seeking out sources and patiently and meticulously answering my every question, often the same question over and over. Deficiencies that remain must, however, be laid at my door. It might be, for example, that a certain intensity in some place has eluded me.

The notes draw on Japanese critical and biographical scholarship, in particular that of Yoshida Seiichi in *Akutagawa Ryũnosuke shũ* (Tokyo, Kadokawa Shoten, 1970), with some new putting two and two together observations.

I am also indebted to XAVIER KALCK for discussions about French references and to KIUCHI KUMIKO for introducing me to Akutagawa's essay "About Myself at That Time" in which he writes: "Overall the department of 'pure literature' is such a strange 'business.'"

ANTHONY BARNETT

Note on Transliteration

The wavy circumflex ˜ [not the tilde of similar form] is used here in place of the conventional macron ˉ, an ugly sort, to denote a long vowel though omitted in naturalized Tokyo. Long vowels are pronounced as short but held twice the duration. Some transliterations double the vowel to denote length but this creates confusion because pronunciation is closer to oh than ooh. An anomoly is the bashõ tree given in 15. "Them" as basjoo, the common botanical name by which it is known in European languages. Distinguishing the long vowel is not unimportant because basho does not have the same meaning as bashõ/basjoo. French uses the circumflex ˆ to denote a long vowel. A final e is always sounded.

I LEAVE entirely to you the responsibility to decide not only whether this manuscript should be published, but also when and where.

I suspect you know most of the people who make an appearance here. However, if it is published, I would rather you did not add an index.

I am living now in the most unhappy happiness. But strange to say I have no regrets. I just feel sorry for those who have had such a bad husband, child, parent as I am. So now, Goodbye. I do not believe I have defended myself here, at least not *consciously*.

Finally, the reason I leave this manuscript with you is because I think you know me probably better than anyone else. (If only to strip away my skin as an urbanite) in reading this manuscript please laugh at how foolish I am.

Shōwa 2, June 20 [20 June 1927]

AKUTAGAWA RYŪNOSUKE

TO MY DEAR FRIEND KUME MASAO

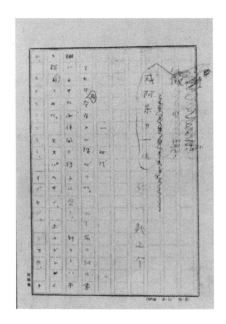

1. THE AGE

It was on the first floor of a bookshop. Twenty years old, he climbed a European-style ladder leaning against the bookshelves, looking for new books. Maupassant, Baudelaire, Strindberg, Ibsen, Shaw, Tolstoy . . .

Meanwhile sunset was fast approaching. But he carried on regardless, intent on reading the letters on the spines of the books. More than books, *fin de siècle* itself was arrayed there. Nietzsche, Verlaine, the brothers Goncourt, Dostoevsky, Hauptmann, Flaubert . . .

Struggling against the twilight, he took stock of their names. But the books themselves began to sink into melancholy shadows. Tired out at last he prepared to start down the European-style ladder. Just then an unshaded light bulb, directly above his head, lit up. Perched on the ladder, he looked down at the salesclerks and the customers. They appeared strangely small. Indeed, quite wretched.

"Life is not worth a single line of Baudelaire."

For a while, from the ladder, he looked upon people such as these. . . .

2. MOTHER

The lunatics were all made to wear the same mouse-coloured clothes. Accordingly, the large room seemed to look even more melancholic. One of them was at the organ fervently intent on playing a hymn. At the same time one of them stood in the middle of the room, jumping about rather than dancing.

He was watching scenes like these in the company of a ruddy complexioned doctor. His mother, ten years earlier, had been no different from them. Not in the slightest—in fact, he could smell his mother in their smell.

"Well, shall we go?"

The doctor led the way and entered a room down the corridor. In a corner of the room a number of brains were immersed in alcohol in large glass jars. He discovered a pale white substance on one of them. It resembled a few drops of egg-white. Standing chatting with the doctor, he again remembered his mother.

"The owner of this brain was a man, an engineer with the X X Electricity Company. He used to think of himself as a huge dynamo, black sparking."

He was looking out the window, avoiding the doctor's eyes. There was nothing there but a brick wall embedded with pieces of empty bottles. But blearily they whitened the sparse moss.

3. HOUSE

His was living in a first floor room in a suburb. It was a first floor oddly canting because of the unstable ground.

In this first floor flat his aunt was often quarrelling with him. Sometimes he could not do without his adoptive parents' intervention. Yet he loved his aunt more than anyone. A spinster all her life, his aunt was almost an elderly sixty while he was no more than twenty.

In this room in a suburb, many times he even thought that those who love each other cause each other misery. Along with such thoughts, he felt the eerie cant of the first floor.

4. TOKYO

The River Sumida was leaden overcast. From the window of the small steamer under way he was viewing the cherry blossoms on Mukōjima. To his eyes, cherry trees in blossom were melancholy, like a line of rag cloth. But somewhere in the cherries—Mukōjima cherries dating from the Edo Period—he found himself.

5. SELF

Seated with his elder at a café table, he was smoking roll-ups non-stop. He hardly opened his mouth. But he listened intently to his elder's words.

"Today I spent half the day in the automobile."

"Did you have some business to see to?"

His elder, propping his cheek, answered quite off-hand.

"Oh, I just felt like riding around."

The words released him into an unknown world—a world of his "Self" close to the gods. He felt some pain. But, also, pleasure.

The café was just a tiny box. But under a framed god of Pan a gum tree planted in an ochre pot bore fleshy leaves.

6. Illness

In a steady sea breeze, he opened wide a large English-language dictionary, looking for words with his fingertips.

Talaria	Winged boots or sandals
Tale	A story
Talipot	An East-Indian palm 50 to 100 feet high. The leaves are borne as umbrellas and are used also for making hats and fans, etc. It flowers once every 70 years . . .

His imagination clearly depicted the flowers of this palm. Then, feeling a hitherto unknown itching in his throat, he found himself spitting phlegm onto the dictionary. Phlegm? —But it wasn't phlegm. Thinking of a brief life, he once again imagined the flowers of this palm. Beyond this faraway sea, palm flowers soaring high.

7. PAINTING

He, suddenly—it was that sudden. Standing in front of a bookshop, looking at a book of Van Gogh's paintings, he suddenly understood what painting was. Of course, the book of paintings must be no more than a photographic version. But even in that photographic version he felt nature vividly surfacing.

This passion of his for paintings restored his perspective. He found himself paying undivided attention to the undulation of a tree bough or the soft roundness of a woman's cheek.

In the dusk, one lowering autumn evening, he was walking under an iron girder bridge in a suburb. Below the bank on the far side of the bridge a cart was standing. Passing by he had the feeling that someone had passed this way before. Who? —It wasn't even necessary to ask himself any longer.

In his twenty-three-year-old mind, a Dutchman, ear severed, long-stem pipe in his mouth, cast piercing eyes over this melancholic landscape. . . .

8. SPARKS

Drenched in rain he was treading the asphalt. The rain was pelting down. Among the plentiful splashes he caught the smell of his vulcanized coat.

There in front of his eyes an overhead cable was discharging violet sparks. He was strangely moved. His jacket pocket concealed his manuscript for publication in the coterie magazine. Walking in the downpour, he turned to look up once more at the cable.

The cable was still discharging keen sparks. Looking over his life, there was nothing in particular he wanted. Only these violet sparks, —only this wild aerial display of sparks, which he wanted to catch, even if it meant sacrificing his life.

9. CADAVERS

Every cadaver had a label attached to a wire hanging from a thumb. And those labels were written on with such details as names and ages. His friend, bending over, skillfully moving his scalpel, started to peel the skin from the face of a cadaver. Spreading out underneath the skin was beautiful yellow fat.

He was looking at the body. Indeed, he had to in order to finish a short story, —a short story whose background drew on some dynastic period. But the stench of the cadaver, something like rotted apricots, was sickening. His friend, knitting his brow, went on silently moving his scalpel.

"These days even cadavers are hard to come by."

His friend was telling him this. Before he realized it, he had his answer ready. —"If I were short of a cadaver, without any malice aforethought, I would commit murder." But, of course, his answer was only in his head.

10. MENTOR

Under the great oak he was reading his mentor's book. The oak in the autumn sunlight stirred not even a single leaf. Somewhere far away in the air a balance hung with glass cups keeps just equilibrium. —Reading his mentor's book, he sensed such a scene. . . .

11. DAWN

The night was gradually giving way to dawn. He found himself on a street corner looking out over a huge market. The people and the vehicles crowding the market were beginning to be tinted with a rosy hue.

He lit a roll-up and silently made his way into the market. Then, suddenly, a scrawny black dog, barking at him. But he was not taken aback. Moreover he was in love even with that dog.

In the middle of the market, a sycamore was spreading its branches in all four directions. Standing at its foot, he looked up beyond the branches at the soaring sky. In the sky just above him a star was shining.

It was his twenty-fifth year, —three months since he met his mentor.

12. Naval Harbor

Inside the submarine it was half-dark. Bending low among the surrounding machinery front and back, left and right he was looking into a small glass. And then reflected on the glass a bright naval harborscape.

"You can see the *Kongō* out there, too."

It was a naval officer who was speaking to him. Viewing the small warship on the square lens, for no reason Holland parsley came to mind. The faint aroma of parsley on a mere plate of beefsteak at 30 sen per portion.

13. MENTOR'S DEATH

In the wind after the rain he was walking down the platform of a new station. The sky was still half-dark. Beyond the platform, three or four railway workers, lifting and lowering their pickaxes in unison, were singing in a shrill voice.

The wind after the rain tore through the workers' song or his emotions. His roll-up unlit he was feeling an anguish close to exaltation. The telegram MENTOR CRITICAL crushed into the pocket of his coat. . . .

Just then from behind the pine hills, the 6 a.m. up train, a weaving line, approached trailing a wisp of smoke.

14.   MARRIAGE

The second day of their marriage, "It's a trouble to be wasting money right after coming here," he chided his wife. But rather than his own chiding it was his aunt's chiding him "to tell her." His wife was apologizing of course to him, but also to his aunt. A pot of yellow jonquil she had bought for him there in front of her. . . .

15. THEM

They lived peacefully. In the shade of large spreading basjoo leaves. — Because their house was in a costal town a full hour from Tokyo by steam train even.

16. PILLOW

Pillowed on rose leaf scented skepticism, he was reading a book by Anatole France. But he had not realized that half-human half-horse gods were now also already in that pillow.

17. BUTTERFLY

In a breeze filled with the scent of waterweed a butterfly was fluttering. Only for a moment, on his dry lips he felt this butterfly's wing touch. But, some years later only the wing-dust once brushed on his lips was still glittering.

18. MOON

In a hotel, midway on the stairs, he happened to encounter her. Her face seemed as if in the moonlight even by day. Seeing her off (they had never made acquaintance) he felt a loneliness he had never known. . . .

19. Artificial Wings

He moved from Anatole France to the 18th century philosophers. But Rousseau he did not approach. Partly perhaps this was because one aspect of himself was similar to Rousseau's—too easily driven by passion. He approached the philospher of *Candide* closer to another of his own aspects— an aspect endowed with icy intellect.

Life to his twenty-nine years of age was no longer at all bright. But Voltaire provided a person such as himself with artificial wings.

Spreading these wings, he flew lightly into the sky. Simultaneously life's joys and sorrows bathed in the light of reason sank away beneath his eyes. Letting smiles and ironies fall on shabby towns, he soared through open air straight for the sun. And, just as that ancient Greek with artificial wings like these burned by sunlight finally fell to sea and died, forgot. . . .

20.   SHACKLES

A couple, they came to live in the same house as his adoptive parents. This was because he went to work for a newspaper publisher. He was depending on a contract written on a sheet of yellow paper. But, looking later at the contract, the newspaper publisher was not under any obligation. He alone was obligated.

21. Mad Girl

Two rickshaws were running along an empty overcast country road. That the road led to the sea was quite evident from the arrival of the sea breeze. He, seated on the rear rickshaw, suspicious of his utter lack of interest in this rendezvous, was wondering what had brought him here. It was not passion at all. If not passion, —to avoid answering, "At any rate we are equals," he could not help thinking.

The one seated on the front rickshaw was a mad girl. Not only that, her younger sister had killed herself out of jealousy.

"Now there's nothing to be done."

For this mad girl—she, who was driven only by strong animal instincts—he was already feeling a hatred.

Meanwhile the two rickshaws were skirting a cemetery smelling of ocean. Inside a hedge fence of woven branches and oyster shells numerous cairns were blackened. Looking out over a faintly shining sea beyond them, suddenly inexplicably her husband, —he began to feel contempt for her husband incapable of holding her heart. . . .

22. A PAINTER

It was an illustration in a magazine. Nevertheless, this sumi-e of a cock displayed extraordinary individuality. He enquired of one of his friends about this painter.

A week or so later, this painter visited him. It was one of the most momentous events of his life. In this painter he discovered his self, which was unknown to anyone. Moreover he discovered his soul, which he himself had not known.

One autumn evening, with a nip in the air, from a stalk of Indian corn he suddenly remembered this painter. The tall corn, coarse-leaf armoured, was exposing ever so thinly nerve-like its roots above the lifted earth. Surely that must also be his own self-portrait of his vulnerable self. But such a discovery only made him melancholy.

"Too late. But when it comes to the point . . ."

23. HER

Evening was closing in in front of a square. His body a little feverish, he was walking across this square. The big buildings, many of them, glowed with electric lights from their windows in the faintly silver lucid sky.

He stopped at the kerb-side, deciding to wait for her. Some five minutes later she walked up to him, looking rather haggard. But, on seeing his face, "I'm just tired," she said, managing a smile. Shoulder to shoulder, they were walking across the square in the twilight. This was the first time for them. To be with her he felt capable of abandoning everything.

After getting into their car, gazing intently at his face, she said, "You won't regret, will you?" Decisively, "I won't regret," he answered. Pressing his hand, "I won't regret, and you," she said. Her face even at such a moment looked as if in the moonlight.

24. Childbirth

Standing awhile beside the fusuma, he was looking down at the midwife in her white delivery gown washing a baby. The baby, whenever soap made its eyes smart, wrinkled its piteous face. Moreover it kept up its high-pitched bawl. Catching a rather pinkie-like baby smell, he could not help thinking acutely like this. —

"For what has this mite also been born? Into this world filled with suffering and afflictions. —For what in the world has this mite been burdened with the fate of a father like me?"

Not only that it was the first boy his wife had given birth to.

25. STRINDBERG

He was standing in the doorway of his room watching some two-bit Chinamen playing mahjong in the pomegranate blossom moonlight. Then back inside the room, under a low lamp, he began reading *The Confession of a Fool*. But, before reading even two pages he found himself giving a wry smile. —Strindberg in his letters to his lover, the Baroness, is also writing lies not so different from his. . . .

26. ANTIQUITY

Discoloured buddhas, celestial beings, horses, lotus flowers almost over-whelmed him. Gazing up at them, he had forgotten everything. Even his own good fortune in escaping the hands of that mad girl. . . .

He was walking with his friend down a back street. There a hooded rickshaw was heading straight toward them, from there. Unexpectedly, moreover, the person on it was she of last night. Her face, even in such daylight, looked as if in moonlight. In the presence of his friend, of course, they did not even exchange a greeting.

"A beauty, isn't she?"

His friend was remarking. Keeping his eyes on the spring mountains at the end of the street, without hesitation he replied.

"Yes, quite a beauty."

28.   MURDER

The country road in the sunlight was smelling of cow dung. Wiping away sweat, he was toiling up the hill slope. On both sides, ripened barley was giving off its sweet scent.

"Kill, kill. . . ."

He found himself mouthing this word over and over. Whom? —To him, it was self-evident. He was remembering an altogether obsequious-like short-cropped man.

Just then beyond the yellowed barley the edifice of a Roman Catholic cathedral, all of a sudden, began to reveal its dome. . . .

29. FORM

It was an iron sake flask. There was a moment when this thread pattern flask had taught him the beauty of "form."

30. RAIN

He was on a big bed talking with her about this and that. Outside the bedroom window it was raining. The rugosa rose in this rain seemed to have been rotting awhile. Her face as always seemed to be as if in the moonlight. Yet, talking with her was not untiresome to him. Lying on his stomach, silently lighting a roll-up, he remembered it was already seven years since he had begun to live with her.

"Do I love this woman?"

He asked himself. This answer was unexpected even to himself who had been observing himself.

"I still love her."

It was like the smell of overripe apricots. Walking among the charred ruins, he faintly caught this smell, and even thought the smell of corpses rotting under a blazing sky was not altogether bad. And yet, on coming up to the edge of the pond where corpses were piled and piled up, he discovered the expression "noseburn" to be no sensory exaggeration at all. What especially moved him was the corpse of a twelve- or thirteen-year-old child. Watching this corpse, he felt something akin to envy. "Those whom the gods love die young"—such words also entered his head. The houses of both his sister and his younger brother with a different mother had burned down. As for his sister's husband he had been given a suspended sentence for committing perjury. . . .

"Better if everyone were dead."

Standing still in the charred ruins, he could not help such deep-rooted thoughts.

32. A FIGHT

He scuffled with his younger brother with a different mother. His brother because of him must have been easily under pressure. Equally, he too because of his brother must have lost his liberty. His relatives were always telling his brother to "follow his example." But to himself this was like being bound hand and foot. Locked in a scuffle, they ended up rolling onto the veranda. In the garden along the veranda one-hundred-day myrtle, —he remembers it even now. —Under a lowering sky a profusion of red blushing flowers.

33. Hero

From the window of Voltaire's house, he found himself gazing up at a high mountain. Above the glaciated mountain peak not even the shadow of a vulture was to be seen. But a short Russian was resolutely climbing a mountain path.

When night had also closed in on Voltaire's house, under a bright lamp he tried his hand at writing a left-wing poem like this.

Remembering the figure of a Russian climbing that mountain path. . . .

—You who more than anyone kept the Ten Commandments
more than anyone you broke the Ten Commandments.

You who more than anyone loved the populace
more than anyone you despised the populace.

You who more than anyone blazed with ideals
more than anyone you knew reality.

You are the flower scented electric locomotive
to whom our Orient has given birth. —

34. COLOURS

Thirty years old, he found he was in love with a vacant lot. There on the mossy growth only bits and pieces of brick and tile, many of them, were strewn about. But to his eyes it was no different from a landscape by Cézanne.

His passions of seven or eight years ago flashed across his mind. And now he also discovered that seven or eight years ago he had not understood colours.

35. Motley Puppet

Not to have any regrets whenever he would die, he was determined to live an intense life. In fact, he was still leading a modest life in deference to his adoptive parents and his aunt. This brought aspects of both light and dark into his life. Seeing a motley puppet standing in a Western clothes shop, he thought how like a motley puppet he could be. But, out of his consciousness he himself—his second self, so to speak—had already incorporated this state of mind in a short story.

36. LASSITUDE

With a university student he was walking in a field of silver grass.

"You still have a vigorous appetite for living, don't you?"

"Yes, —but even you do too . . ."

"Quite the opposite, I do not. I do have an appetite to be productive, though."

This was his true feeling. He had in fact lost interest in life somewhere along the way.

"Surely an appetite to be productive is an appetite for living, isn't it."

He did not answer at all. The field of grass above its red ears had begun to reveal a volcano. For this volcano he felt something akin to envy. But he himself did not know why. . . .

He encountered a woman able to combat him even in intellectual strength. In writing "One from Yonder" and other lyric poems he barely escaped this crisis. It was heartrending as if brushing off something frozen on a tree trunk, shining snow.

> Whirling in the wind a sedge hat ˄
> Why shouldn't it fall by the way
> How can my name be a regret
> Regretted is your name only

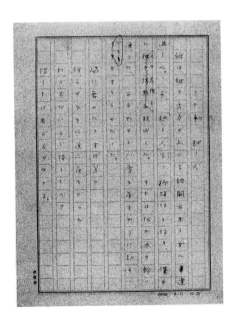

38. Vengeance

It was on a hotel balcony among trees in bud. He was drawing there, letting a boy play beside him. The only son of a mad girl with whom he had completely severed relations seven years before.

The mad girl, lighting a roll-up, was watching them play. With a heavy heart, he went on drawing a locomotive or an aeroplane. Fortunately, the boy was not his child. But to him, being called "uncle" was what was most distressing.

After the boy had wandered off, the mad girl, smoking her roll-up, spoke to him coquettishly.

"That boy is like you, isn't he?"

"Not like me. In the first place . . ."

"But there's prenatal training, isn't there."

He turned away in silence. But in the depths of his mind not even the absence of a cruel desire, to strangle this girl such as she was.

39. MIRRORS

He was talking with his friend in a corner of a café. His friend, eating a baked apple, talked about the recent cold, and so on. In the midst of such talk, he suddenly sensed contradictions.

"You're still single, aren't you?"

"No, getting married next month."

In spite of himself, he was lost for words. Inlaid mirrors on the café walls were reflecting his countless selves. Chillingly, almost threateningly. . . .

Why do you attack the existing social system?

Because I see the evils capitalism has engendered.

Evils? I didn't think you saw any difference between good and evil. Then, what about your life?

—Just so he held a dialogue with an angel. With an angel who wears a silk hat who shouldn't be ashamed of anyone. . . .

He began to suffer insomnia. Moreover his physical strength also started to ebb. Several doctors each made two or three diagnoses of his illness. —Hyperacidity, gastric atony, dry pleurisy, neurasthenia, chronic conjunctivitis, brain fatigue . . .

But he himself knew the root cause of his illness. It was his state of mind feeling ashamed of himself and also his fearing them. Them—the society he had despised!

One snow-clouded cloudy afternoon, he was in a corner of a café with a lighted cigar in his mouth, listening to the music floating across from the gramophone there. It was a music that strangely permeated his mind. Waiting for the music to finish, he walked over to the gramophone in order to study the label on the record.

The Magic Flute—Mozart

All of a sudden he understood. Mozart who had broken the Ten Commandments must indeed have suffered. Just like him . . . bending his head low, he made his way silently back to his table.

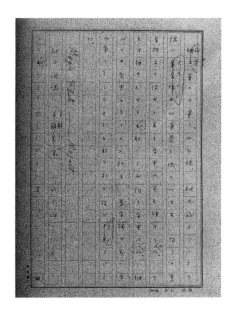

42.   LAUGHTER OF THE GODS

Thirty-five years old he was walking among pines slant-lit by the spring sun. Remembering the words "Unfortunately for them, unlike us, the Gods cannot kill themselves" he himself had written two or three years earlier. . . .

43. Night

Once again night was closing in. In the faint light the wild-looking sea incessantly broke its spray. Under such a sky, for a second time, he was wedded to his wife. It was a joy for them. But at the same time a torment. Their three children, together with them, were watching the lightning out at sea. His wife, one of the children in her arms, seemed to be holding back her tears.

"Over there you can see a boat, can't you?"

"Yes."

"A boat with its mast broken in two."

44. DEATH

Fortunate to be sleeping alone, looping his sash over the window frame, he tried to strangle himself. But, on slipping his head through the sash, he suddenly began to be afraid of death. It was not because of the agony on the verge of death that he was afraid. He decided, making a second attempt to strangle himself, to hold his pocket watch. Then, after feeling a moment's agony, everything began to blur. Once past this stage, he must surely enter into death. Checking the hands of his watch, he found he had experienced agony for about a minute and twenty seconds. Pitch dark outside the window frame. But in the darkness the wild crowing of a cock was also audible.

Divan tried to give new strength to his mind once again. This was the "Eastern Goethe" he had not known. Seeing Goethe on the far shore standing confidentally beyond all good and evil, he felt an envy bordering on despair. The poet Goethe in his eyes was greater than the poet Christ. In this poet's soul not only the Acropolis or Golgotha but the rose of Araby flowered. If only he had strength enough to follow in this poet's footsteps, —After he had finished reading Divan and its awesome impact had subsided he could not help deeply despising himself, he who was born a eunuch at life.

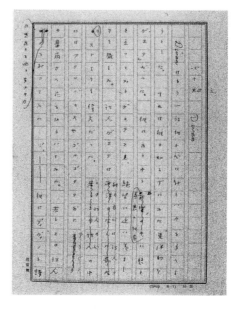

46. LIES

The suicide of his sister's husband came as a blow. This time he had to take care of his sister's family. His future, at least as far as he could see, was as dim as twilight. Feeling almost like deriding his mental bankruptcy, (knowing all there was to know about his vices and his weaknesses . . .) he carried on as usual reading various books. But even Rousseau's *Confessions* was full of heroic lies. Especially that *New Life*—a more wily hypocrite he had never met than the protagonist of *New Life*. Just François Villon alone penetrated his soul. He discovered the "beautiful male" in some of those poems.

Villon, waiting for the hangman, sometimes appeared in his dreams too. Like Villon he tried many times to sink to the depths of life. But his circumstances and physical energy did not permit such a thing. Slowly he wasted away. Like a tree withering from the top, as Swift had once seen. . . .

She had a radiant face. It was as if the morning sun cast its light on a thin sliver of ice. He had a liking for her. But he did not feel a passion. Nor had he laid even a finger on her body.

"You want to die, don't you, that's what I heard."

"Yes. —No, tired of living rather than want to die."

Out of such a dialogue, they vowed to die together.

"'Platonic suicide,' isn't it?"

"'Double platonic suicide.'"

He could not help wondering why he himself was so composed.

48. Death

He did not die with her. Simply the fact that he had not even laid a finger on her body was somehow satisfaction enough. Sometimes she talked with him as if nothing had happened. Moreover, handing him a phial of cyanide, she even said, "Now that we have this both of us can be strong."

Actually, it did strengthen his resolve. Sitting alone in a rattan chair, looking at young chinquapin leaves, often he could not help thinking of the peace death would bring him.

49. MOUNTED SWAN

Exhausting all his inner resources, he set about trying to write his autobiography. But, it did not come to him as easily as he had imagined. It was because his self-esteem, scepticism, or calculation of interests, still remained. He could not help despising such qualities in himself. On the other hand he also could not help thinking "everyone is the same under the skin." For him the title of the book *Poetry and Truth* could just as well be the title of any autobiography. Moreover, it was evident to him that literary works did not necessarily move everyone. The people to whom his works appeal must be no one other than those close to him who live a life close to his. —Such was the feeling at work on him. That was why he decided to try his hand briefly at his own *Poetry and Truth.*

After writing up *A Fool's Life*, he happened upon a mounted swan in a second-hand shop. Although it was standing with its neck held high, even its yellowed feathers were worm-eaten. Thinking of his own life, he felt tears and derision welling up. Before him was only insanity or suicide. He walked along the street in the twilight, quite alone, determined to await the fate that was gradually coming to annihilate him.

One of his friends went mad. Towards this friend he had always felt a particular attachment. It was because more than anyone else he understood this friend's loneliness, —the loneliness under his jaunty mask. He visited this friend two or three times after he went mad.

"You and I are possessed by a demon. By the so-called demon of *fin de siècle*, aren't we."

This friend, dropping his voice to a whisper, spoke these things to him. But, two or three days later, it was told that on his way to a hot-spring lodge he was eating even rose flowers. After this friend was hospitalized, he remembered the terracotta bust he had once given him. It was a bust of the author of *The Inspector* whom this friend loved. He remembered that Gogol also died insane and he could not help feeling some force governing them.

On the point of utter exhaustion, he happened to read Radiguet's dying words, and once again he felt the laughter of the gods. They were the words "The soldiers of God are coming to seize me." He tried to fight against his superstition and his sentimentalism. Any fight was, however, *physically* impossible for him. In fact, the "demon of *fin de siècle*" must be tormenting him. He envied those people of the Middle Ages who found strength in God. But to believe in God—to believe in the love of God was utterly impossible for him. The God in which even that Cocteau believed!

51. DEFEAT

In him the one hand holding the pen started to tremble. Moreover even saliva started to run. His head, except on waking after taking 0.8 Veronal, cleared not once. Even then it was clear for no more than half an hour or an hour. He was barely scraping a living day by day in semi-darkness. So to speak, an edge nicked, fine sword for a stick.

LETTER

KUME MASAO (1891–1952), writer, Akutagawa's friend since student days. Some scholars believe it was not Akutagawa's intention that it be published. Inevitably, most editions carry extensive annotations, despite his wish that no index be added. Readers who do not like biographical intrusions should pass over these notes while those who would like more information can turn, for example, to the apparatus in the 2006 Penguin selection *Rashōmon and Seventeen Other Stories*, which also includes other autobiographical pieces. For critical comment on the Penguin translation see especially "Introduction" and notes to 24. "Childbirth" and 25. "Strindberg".

1. THE AGE

The bookshop is Maruzen. Akutagawa writes "Western-style ladder", here rendered "European-style". Akutagawa correctly writes *fin de siècle*, not *la fin du siècle*, curiously given in the French translation, which means something else: the last decade of any century. Other translations give "the *fin de siècle*", which diminishes a significant unorthodox stand alone use of this adjectival phrase—see also 50. Captive.

2. MOTHER

NIIHARA [née AKUTAGAWA] FUKU (1850–1902). Akutagawa's mother went insane in 1892. She was kept mainly hidden away in her house until her death. In 1892 Akutagawa went to live in the household of his mother's brother AKUTAGAWA DŌSHŌ (1849–1928) and his wife TOMO (1857–1937). He was formally adopted in 1904. Not until then was his name legally Akutagawa. Akutagawa revealed his mother's insanity in public for the first time in 1926 in the story "Tenbiko", first translated in the 2006 Penguin selection as "Death Register".

Perhaps Tokyo's Aoyama Hospital or Nagasaki Prefectural Hospital. Akutagawa visited Nagasaki in 1919 establishing a lifelong friendship with the tanka poet SAITŌ MOKICHI (1882–1953) who was then chief psychiatrist of the latter before becoming director of the Aoyama, though Saitō may not be the doctor referred to here: "Ten years earlier" either dates Akutagawa's hospital visit *c.*1912 at the latest—his mother died in 1902—or is poetic license. The second edition of Saitō's 1913 collection *Shakkō* features in Akatagawa's *Haguruma* [*Cogwheels*]—see "Introduction" for translations. A selection from *Shakkō* has been translated as *Red Lights* (West Lafayette, Purdue, 1989)—see also 9. "Cadavers" and notes to 50. "Captive" and 51. "Defeat".

3. HOUSE

AUNT FUKI (1856–1938), his mother's unmarried sister—for her sister FUYU see note to 32. "A Fight". The flat was in a house on farm premises in the then suburb of Shinjuku, now a central part of Tokyo.

4. TOKYO

Mukōjima is an area on the east bank of the River Sumida famous for cherry blossom viewing. Edo was renamed Tokyo at the time of the Meiji Restoration in 1868.

5. SELF

TANIZAKI JUN'ICHIRŌ (1886–1965), writer, many of whose works are available in English.

6. ILLNESS

In May 1915 Akutagawa thought he had tuberculosis but tests proved negative—see also 41. "Illness". Akutagawa owned the heavy two-volume *Funk & Wagnalls New Standard Dictionary of the English Language*. For *Talaria* and *Tale* he translates directly into Japanese parts of *F & G* entries. For *Talaria*, *F & G* gives the near tautology "Winged boots or sandals", though continues "or sometimes wings appearing to spring directly from the ankles." The *F & G* entry for *Tale* is, of course, more expansive than "A story". For *Talipot* Akutagawa directly translates part and adapts part, giving "The leaves are made into umbrellas, fans, hats, etc." The present translator goes back to *F & G*'s "The leaves are borne as umbrellas and are used also for making hats and fans", while keeping Akutagawa's "etc." Akutagawa replaces botanical information about leaves with vital information about flowering not given in *F & G*.

The "talipot palm", *Corypha* native to East-India, is not the "coconut palm", *Cocos* native to Polynesia, given in another translation, which mistakes a general Japanese word, roughly equivalent to English "palm", to mean specifically the "coconut palm", to which the Japanese word is also commonly applied.

8. SPARKS

The kanji for "sparks" consist of "fire" and "flower". The coterie magazine is *Shin Shichō* [*New Thought*].

9. CADAVERS
The Medical School in Tokyo, which Akutagawa is believed to have visited while writing "Rashō Gate", believed to be the story referred to here, of which there are at least five English translations.

10. MENTOR
NATSUME SŌSEKI (1867–1916), writer, many of whose works are available in English. He is known by his pen personal name Sōseki. Akutagawa surely saw Sōseki as a father figure, not just his mentor.

12. NAVAL HARBOR
Akutagawa taught English for a while at the Yokosuka Naval Engineering College. His story "Bunshō", first translated in the 2006 Penguin selection as "The Writer's Craft", stems from this experience. *Kongō* is a now archaic word for "diamond". Parsley available in Japan at the time was known as *oranda zeri*, "Dutch parsley." The sen is a now obsolete unit of currency. There were 100 sen to the yen.

13. MENTOR'S DEATH
Akutagawa was in the coastal town of Kamakura and did not get back to Tokyo before Sōseki's death on 9 December 1916. Akutagawa presided over the reception at the Aoyama Funeral Hall service.

14. MARRIAGE
Akutagawa married TSUKAMOTO FUMI (1900–1968) on 2 February 1918. His Aunt Fuki lived with them in Kamakura for a few months at first, taking on the role of mother-in-law.

15. THEM
Basjoo is a common botanical name in European laguages for the bashō tree or Japanese fibre banana (inedible) of the plantain family, from which the haiku poet Bashō took his pen personal name.

17. BUTTERFLY
Some commentators believe the butterfly refers to the mad girl of 21. The present translator does not agree. Were it to refer to a woman with whom Akutagawa formed an attachment outside his marriage, the woman of 18, 23 or 27 seems more likely. It could also represent an embodiment of Akutagawa himself. But there is no reason to believe the experience is purely symbolic and not also rooted in reality. The plant implied here is one of fresh water.

18. MOON
The woman whose face seems as if in moonlight—Akutagawa does not write "bathed"—is believed to be NONOGUCHI [née HIGUCHI] YUTAKA, wife of the owner of prestigious Hotel Komaki-en in Kamakura. Such a woman also appears in 23 and 27—though not necessarily the same one. A 1930 reference by Akutagawa's first translator, Glenn W. Shaw, suggests that the poet KUJŌ TAKEKO (1887–1928), regarded as an ideal woman of modern Japan, may be one. If not, Shaw nevertheless was given to understand that Akutagawa was deeply affected by her toward the end of his life. Contextually, the woman whose face seems as if in the moonlight in 30 should be Akutagawa's wife.

19. ARTIFICIAL WINGS
Akutagawa writes "burned". In the myth of Icarus the wax holding the wings together melted.

20. SHACKLES
The newspaper is the *Ōsaka Mainichi Shinbun*, Tokyo office, with which Akutagawa was already associated. His new contract gave him a smallish regular monthly salary with no additional manuscript fees. He was, though, free to publish stories elsewhere in magazines but not to write for other newspapers.

21. MAD GIRL
HIDE SHIGEKO (1890–1973), poet whom Akutagawa met in 1919, with whom he had a deeply painful affair, though apparently they were intimate just once. Falsely, she told Akutagawa that he was the father of her second child born in 1921. The father was, in fact, her husband, an engineer, who is probably the obsequious-like man of 28. "Murder"—see also 26. "Antiquity" and 38. "Vengeance".

22. A PAINTER
OANA RYUICHI (1894–1966), who came to illustrate covers to many of Akutagawa's books. "In this painter he discovered his self, which was unknown to anyone." Early editions print the kanji for "poetry", which many scholars now believe is a perpetuated error from an apparent mistake in Akutagawa's manuscript, i.e. "In this painter he discovered a poetry unknown to anyone." Since the 1970s some editions print the kanji for "self" and this is what is preferred here. It would be rash to

express certainty but it is hard to believe that Akutagawa intended to write "poetry", which is quite a banality in this context in itself, the more so in light of "soul" in the next sentence: "Moreover he discovered his soul, which he himself had not known." He would too be claiming immodestly that he alone had discovered "poetry" in Oana.

23. HER & 27. SPARTAN DISCIPLINE & 30. RAIN
See note to 18. "Moon".

24. CHILDBIRTH
First boy: HIROSHI (1920–1981), actor and director—see also note to 43. "Night".
Akutagawa writes the Japanese for "baby mouse", for which English has an excellent word in "pinkie". It is not the "rat", symptomatic, of the 2006 Penguin selection.
Akutagawa writes "shabaku" which means "sahā suffering". Naturally, Buddhist "shaba", or "shaba sekai", has wider secular currency in Japanese than has Sanskrit "sahā", or "sahā world", in English.

25. STRINDBERG
Akutagawa writes "dirty Chinamen", here rendered "two-bit Chinamen".
Strindberg wrote his autobiographical fiction *le Plaidoyer d'un fou* [*Plea . . . Madman* or *Fool*] in French but he also sold the manuscript to a German publisher. A mutilated German version *Die Beichte eines Thoren* [*The Confession of a Fool*] appeared first. The Japanese version available to Akutagawa, slightly revised in 1923, was originally translated from the German. Strindberg's first English translator, while acknowledging in her introduction the deficiences of the German edition, nevertheless also took over the German title. Akutagawa certainly owned the English version. He said that his knowledge of French was not as good. There have been corrective translations since: the German *Plädoyer eines Irren* [*Plea . . . Madman*], the English *A Madman's Defence*. Swedish translations, not by Strindberg, of which there have been three, are all entitled *En dåres försvarstel* [*A Madman's Defence*—"försvarstel" can be translated "plea" but unlike "plaidoyer" it is not the juristic word for "plea".] All Japanese versions retain the title translated from the German. Even if Akutagawa knew the French edition, he nevertheless uses the kanji for "fool" and "confession", not "madman" and "plea / defence". The only acceptable English translation of Akutagawa's Japanese is *The Confession of a Fool*—with *Confession* in the singular, a distinction that does not exist in Japanese—see fol. It need hardly be said that Strindberg's title, in its compromised form, has great significance for Akutagawa's own. Whether "fou" is "fool" or "madman"—he also knew Gogol's *Diary of a Madman*, in French *le Journal d'un fou* and, no doubt, St Paul, Erasmus, Voltaire on folly—it is not the "stupid man" of the 2006 Penguin selection, which in giving, though incorrectly in the plural, *The Confessions of a Fool* also gives the lie to "stupid". Further evidence, though none is needed, in support of "fool" is provided by Akutagawa in a mondo— a Zen Buddhist master and student dialogue—in another posthumously published piece "Anchu Mondo" ["Mondo in the Dark"]: "Maybe, you are a fool." "That's right. Maybe I am a fool. Books like *The Confession of a Fool* were written by fools like myself."—translated by Beongcheong Yu as "Dialogue in Darkness", *The East-West Review*, iv/1 (Kyōto, 1971).
German, English and Japanese versions of Strindberg all correctly translate his lover, his wife-to-be, as "Baroness", so given by Strindberg in his original French, her title acquired through her first marriage, not "Countess" so given by Akutagawa. This appears to be a mistake by Akutagawa, corrected here.

26. ANTIQUITY
Akutagawa visited China, March–July 1921, as special correspondent for the *Ōsaka Mainichi Shinbun*.

28. MURDER
See note to 21. "Mad Girl".

29. FORM
The "thread pattern" is "itome", finely incised horizontal banding.

30. RAIN
Inserted with number after completion of rest of manuscript, which therefore shows 31 also as 30, etc.

31. THE GREAT QUAKE
The Great Kantō Earthquake, 1 September 1923. The pond was located in Tokyo's Yoshiwara pleasure quarter. Akutagawa visted the devastation with the writers KON TŌKŌ (1898-1977), and KAWABATA

YASUNARI (1899–1972) many of whose works are available in English. Separately, the Swiss August Kengelbacher (1894–1971) photographed the devastation and scenes similar to the one described by Akutagawa are posted online by Kengelbacher's son at www.japan-guide.com/a/earthquake/

Japanese "sanbi", placed by Akutagawa in quotes, is an unfamiliar archaism, composed of the kanji for "acid nose", meaning "inconsolable grief", manifested by a burning sensation around the base of the nose, here rendered "noseburn". Although carrying a different but contextually not inappropriate connotation, it matches the Japanese in as much as it is a real expression, composed of two ordinary words with an uncommonly-known meaning: "noseburn" and "burn nose" are common names for *Daphnopsis americana* [aka *Daphnopsis tenuifolia*], a spurge-laurel, native to Hawaii and some other islands of tropical America, with an overwhelming caustic stench.

"Those whom the gods love die young": fate of Throphonious and Agamedes in Greek mythology. Whilst Akutagawa's house was not badly damaged, those of his sister HISA (1888–1956) and his half-brother—Akutagawa writes "brother with a different mother"—were destroyed. Hisa's second husband NISHIKAWA YUTAKA (1885–1927) was a lawyer, disbarred and sentenced in 1923 for inciting a client to commit perjury—see also notes to 32. "A Fight" and 46. "Lies".
Akutagawa had another sister HATSU (1885–1891) who died in childhood.

32. A FIGHT
NIIHARA TOKUJI (1898–1930) was Akutagawa's half-brother. His parents were Akutagawa's father and the second sister of Akutagawa's mother AKUTAGAWA FUYU (1862–1920). In 1904, two years after the death of Akutagawa's mother, his father and Aunt Fuyu legalized their relationship.
One-hundred-day myrtle is the present translator's rendering of the crape myrtle referred to here whose kanji mean flowers that bloom for one hundred days.

33. HERO
Lenin, not without sadness, pity even. In his copy of I. D. Levine's *The Man Lenin* (Richmond Hill, NY, 1924) Akutagawa noted "What a comedy". The "left-wing poem" is more motto in form than poem.

35. MOTLEY PUPPET
The story is "Noroma Ningyō" ["Noroma Puppets"], apparently untranslated, in which Akutagawa quotes one of Anatole France's many writings on puppets.

36. LASSITUDE
Silver grasses are varieties of *Miscanthus sinesis* native to China and Japan. Feathery red ears turn silvery white in some varieties. A centre silvery white streak runs the length of the blades in most.

37. ONE FROM YONDER
The Japanese title "Koshibito" means "Person [or "People"] from Koshi". Koshi, which means "The Country Beyond", is the now obsolete name of one of three districts now incorporated under the regional name Hokuriku, which means "North Country". "Yonder" evokes a place name and the beyond—see introduction for a note about the present translator's earlier, wrong, version.
KATAYAMA HIROKO [aka MATSUMURA MINEKO] (1878–1957), poet and translator of Irish literature, with whom Akutagawa fell in love but avoided an affair when they met in Karuizawa in 1924. Katayama was not, in fact, from Koshibito, but nearby.
Akutagawa quotes one of his own poems written in an archaic "Love Letter" form "sōmon": four lines of 7-5 syllables each, here rendered in lines of eight syllables with variable stress, plus hat.

38. VENGEANCE
The artist Oana identifies the setting as the Imperial Hotel, Toyko—see also note to 21. "Mad Girl".

41. ILLNESS
Akutagawa suffered many illnesses throughout his life—see also 6. "Illness".

42. LAUGHTER OF THE GODS
The story, apparently untranslated, is "Maxims of a Midget", in which Akutagawa denigrates himself.

43. NIGHT
Akutagawa and Fumi renewed vows in 1926. Children: HIROSHI (1920–1981), actor and director—see also 24. "Childbirth"; TAKASHI (1922–1945), student draftee killed in Burma—"Kodomo No Byōki", first translated in the 2006 Penguin selection as "The Baby's Sickness", stems from Takashi's hospitalization in 1923; YASUSHI (1925–1989), composer and conductor, who is the child "in her arms".

45. DIVAN

Goethe's *West-oestlicher Divan* (1819, augmented ed., 1826), trans. J. Whaley as *West-Eastern Divan* (London, Wolff, 1974). Apart from the title, Akutagawa writes *Divan* once in German and once in Japanese. From 1926, in particular, Akutagawa studied the Bible, with strong reservations at which "Divan" hints. He was unable to believe in divine miracles or the Judeo-Christian prescription against suicide, which he did not believe was a sin. Indeed, he included Christ in a list of Eastern and Western suicides. On the night of his death Akutagawa completed a manuscript in which he characterized Christ as a poet who had profound insight into everyone but himself—see also note to 51. "Defeat".

46. LIES

Akutagawa's sister Hisa's house was partly destroyed by fire on 4 January 1927. Her second husband, Nishikawa Yutaka, disbarred from practicing law and given a suspended jail sentence for perjury in 1923, was now suspected of arson with a view to insurance fraud. Two days later he threw himself under a train. Hisa remarried her first husband, a vetinarian—see also note to 31. "The Great Quake".

SHIMAZAKI TŌSON (1872–1943), pen personal name Tōson, some of whose works are available in English. He revealed his relationship with his neice, which began after the death of his wife, in his apparently untranslated autobiographical novel *Shinsei* [*New Life*] (1918–1919), in which he appeared to seek to absolve himself. He was criticized for exploiting his family in pursuit of his literary career.

For "beautiful male" Akutagawa writes the kanji for the male of the species in general, implying animalistic physicality; he does not use the kanji for a specifically male human being.

Swift, author of *Gulliver's Travels*, had foreboding of mental decline. Pointing to a tree with a withered crown, he turned to the poet Edward Young, saying: "I shall be like that tree. I shall die from the top." *Gulliver's Travels* was one of several inspirations behind Akutagawa's satirical novel *Kappa* about a civilization of water-dwelling creatures from Japanese mythology.

47. PLAYING WITH FIRE & 48. DEATH

HIRAMATSU MASUKO (1898–1953), unmarried close friend of Akutagawa's wife Fumi, to whom Akutagawa proposed double suicide on 7 April 1927. Hiramatsu informed both Fumi and the artist Oana—see note to 22. "A Painter". Akutagawa was persuaded to abandon the idea.

49. MOUNTED SWAN

Poetry and Truth: subtitle of Goethe's autobiography *Aus meinem Leben: Dichtung und Wahrheit (1811–1833).*

50. CAPTIVE

UNO KŌJI (1891–1961), writer, author of a biographical memoir of Akutagawa, who suffered severe mental breakdown during the years 1927–1933. In June 1927, the month before Akutagawa's suicide, Akutagawa arranged through his psychiatrist friend Saitō Mokichi for Uno to be committed to the Aoyama Hospital—see also notes to 1. "The Age", ref. *fin de siècle*, 2. "Mother" and 51. "Defeat".

Akutagawa writes *The Inspector*. Gogol's play is also known as *The Inspector General, The Government Inspector.* Cocteau in his preface to Raymond Radiguet's posthumously published novel *Le Bal du Comte d'Orgel* (Paris, Grasset, 1924) wrote that Radiguet said: "Dans trois jours je vais être fusillé par les soldats de Dieu." This uses a phrase which in French—not long after World War One—means to be shot by firing squad, here made up of God's soldiers. Violet Schiff's 1952 translation *Count d'Orgel* gives: "In three days I am going to be shot by the soldiers of God." Similarly, Annapaoloa Cancogni's 1989 translation *Count d'Orgel's Ball* gives: "In three days I am going to be shot by God's soldiers." Akutagawa writes "The soldiers of God are coming to seize me." This is retained because it seems to be deliberate. It has not been established whether Akutagawa had access to a Japanese translation.

51. DEFEAT

Akutagawa's 20 June 1927 letter in which he leaves the manuscript of *A Fool's Life* in the care of Kume Masao makes clear that he knew he would commit suicide. He did so with the barbiturate Veronal on 24 July 1927 in the room where his wife and sons were asleep. Despite the precarious state of his health, aggravated by the strain of taking care of his in-laws and his friend Uno, Akutagawa's death was not widely expected among friends, the literary community or his readers. His mood had been cheerful the day before. Akutagawa's family doctor and friend since 1914, SHIMOJIMA ISAO (1870–1947), was called at his death. Akutagawa's pyschiatrist and friend, poet Saitō Mokichi, was shocked to realize that Akutagawa must have used barbiturate prescribed by Saitō—see also notes to 2. "Mother" and 50. "Captive". Akutagawa fell asleep with the Bible beside him—see also note to 45. "Divan". ❡